W
SWALLOWS
RETURN

WHEN SWALLOWS RETURN

A third collection of parables
from farm life in the Welsh mountains

John & Mari Jones

Translated from the Welsh by
Bethan Lloyd-Jones and Kitty Lloyd Jones

BRYNTIRION PRESS

©Evangelical Press of Wales 1992
First published 1992
Bryntirion Press 2010
ISBN 978 1 85049 235 1
(First edition – ISBN 1 85049 107 0)

Designed by Tony Cantale Graphics
Illustrations by Rhiain M. Davies and Ruth Myfanwy
Photographs by W. Arvon Williams
Cover design by Rhiain M. Davies

The original Welsh-language versions of these stories are to be found in the Welsh-language edition of this book, entitled *Daw'r Wennol yn Ôl*.

Published by Bryntirion Press
Bryntirion, Bridgend CF31 4DX
Printed by Gomer Press, Llandysul

CONTENTS

Photographs

1
WHEN SWALLOWS RETURN

This house has been built facing south-east so that we can make the most of what morning sunshine there is – a very welcome luxury on a frosty morning. This amenity has attracted certain visitors to set up home under the eaves of the house and we have the privilege of their company from April right through until autumn.

They are uninvited guests, squatters or non-paying tenants! They build in exactly the same spot year after year and it is no surprise, very early on a summer's morning as we lie in bed, to hear the pleading cries of the hungry nestlings.

Regularly, every year, one nest is built immediately above the front door. Woe betide the caller, patiently waiting for someone to respond to his knock – he may well feel a warm splash down his neck or on his head!

Looking up, he will see busy house-martins darting to and fro, their beaks full of either nest-building material or food for their little ones. Being so busy they have no time to consider the welfare of mere humans!

I have often wondered who taught the chicks – four or five of them to a nest – to keep their home clean from the very first. They either turn their tails towards the opening or over the edge of the nest. And by so doing they make sure that I am kept busy cleaning the window-sill below!

The unfortunate person who dares put his head out of the window of one of the bedrooms close by, will soon be made to feel that he is prying. A high-pitched alarm cry immediately rends the air and in no time at all a flock of parent birds 'home-in', darting to and fro, up and down, among themselves, in noisy protest. They wish to demonstrate that they strongly resent the disturbance of their peace: they stand on their squatters' rights and are prepared to defend them volubly.

Because their diet consists solely of flies they, and many other birds, are forced to bid us farewell at summer's end. You see them in groups chatting together (or so it seems) and planning the return journey to various hot African countries. They must leave in order to survive – they have no choice.

But why do they return here in spring? Is it because

their source of food in Africa is depleted for the remainder of the year? They know from experience how dangerous the journey will be – the number of those that arrive safely is a very small percentage of the number that set out. How strange is this pull of nature! And how do they know when to set out and in which direction to go?

There are certain birds, from countries north of the British Isles, that spend their winters here with us but they invariably return to their native lands for the summer months. Nothing can keep them away. The call of home draws like a magnet.

Experts tell us that the same family, both of fish and birds, returns to the very place where they were born to raise their young. A peculiar urge will drive them back and they will not rest until they reach their destination.

The One who implanted instinct in birds is the One who placed his law in the heart of man. The existence of a divine law deep within, plus the irrefutable testimony of the creation around us (Romans 1:19-20), explains that instinctive feeling that there is something missing, that we lack sustenance, that we are far from home. That feeling is the vestige of that perfect image that was flawed so early in the history of man.

If the creature implicitly follows the instinct planted in its nature by the Creator, should we not expect man to do the same? Regrettably he doesn't. He prefers to seek his sustenance and satisfaction in places so unpromising that his soul starves.

Before man condescends to listen to the divine law the Holy Spirit must stir up an uneasiness within him and create a seeking in his heart. Through the Spirit, through the second birth, we become a new creation (2 Corinthians 5:17). And the result? Like the birds, we shall then be on our way home.

My Father's house on high,
Home of my soul, how near
At times to faith's foreseeing eye
Thy golden gates appear!
Ah! then my spirit faints
To reach the land I love,
The bright inheritance of saints,
Jerusalem above.

JAMES MONTGOMERY

2
'WATCH
THE COWS!'

'I wonder if you could spare a minute? I could really do with some help.' It was a delicate hint that help was needed to move the cows, with their calves, from one field to another. Thinking that I could at least fill a gap, out I went to my appointed task.

'Watch the cows!' That was the only word I had, by way of instruction, and but little did I know at the time what it involved!

The field, which had to be emptied of cows and calves, was on a bit of a slope. Time and time again we thought that we had got them gathered together to the opening at the top end of the field, when, suddenly and without warning, the calves would take it into their heads to rush down-field past us, in a nervous, blind stampede, impossible to restrain – and, invariably of course, they were followed in a wild, panicky rush by their mothers.

Believe me, it was not easy to get ahead of them, while they were aiming for the bottom of the field. They ran at a gallop, tails in the air, with an occasional shake of their body and a sudden leap. They were having a great time provoking us.

If all this is true of cattle, it is doubly true of sheep and lambs. Those are wilder still! When trying to get them into the fold for the first time in the season, the lambs will slip through one's hands in a second. We are always thankful that dogs can be used to make them behave.

But as for cows with young calves, no dog would dare to put in an appearance. He would be just something to be gored and destroyed without delay, before he could begin to look like being the slightest threat to their offspring. And, woe betide anyone who happened to stand between the maddened cow and the dog!

The great secret is to get the cows, or the mother sheep, to remain standing unmoved in their place, even though their progeny should leave them in this wild rush. As surely as the mothers do this, sooner or later, their young will return, calm and in their right minds. But, without a positive stand on the part of the mothers, neither the calves nor the lambs have the faintest idea what is expected of them. The parents' example is the only thing that will make them sober up and come to their senses.

There was a great deal of running around and waving of sticks in the air, that day, and our patience was tried to the limit. It was a continual struggle between us and the frantic cattle, before we finally succeeded in getting them quiet and obedient. No wonder I was given the warning, 'Watch the cows!'

Although the lively cattle had a great time at our expense that day, as we tried to exert our authority over them, we could not but feel that their behaviour would have been very different if they had realized that all we were trying to do was for their good. There was only one purpose to the whole exercise, and that was to move them to better pasture in the other field. But, while each one persisted in going his own way, complete disorder reigned – there was anarchy in the bovine society that afternoon, and life was not too good for them or for us!

'In those days Israel had no king; everyone did as he saw fit' (Judges 17:6). Lawlessness prevailed in the nation of Israel during that period, and at many later times too. And the same is exactly true of us when we reject the claim of God on us. The blame for the present chaos is put on the young, on their parents, on the schools and on religion. But the truth is 'we have turned to our own way'. We have turned our backs on God who wants to lead us into 'green pastures'.

3
THE CARRION CROW

'I saw the devil this morning', said John, on his return from tending the sheep, reminding me, as he said it, of some unusual cries that I had heard, earlier on, from the direction of the field behind the house.

    This was at the end of the lambing season, and John was quite unconcerned that morning, as he went to attend to the sheep. But what should he see in the first field he came to, but one of the last of the ewes to lamb, licking clean her new-born, while a crow – a carrion crow – was dealing with the other end of the lamb! John could hardly believe what he saw; no wonder that he voiced his protest in such unearthly shouts!

He raced to the spot, as fast as his legs could carry him, but it was too late, the deed had been done. The wretched crow had torn the unfortunate little lamb's tongue right out. Poor harmless little creature! What a reception for him as he left the warm world of the womb for such a cruel and pitiless one. However could he suckle without a tongue? It is with his tongue that a lamb pulls at his mother's teats for his life-sustaining milk.

His mother was a two-year-old ewe, enduring birth pains for the first time. In her condition, she did not have the strength necessary to deal with the crow. Otherwise she would have used her feet to stamp, or her head to butt, in an endeavour to drive the crow away. That is all she can do, poor thing, to protect herself and her lamb.

The shepherd knows what is afoot when he sees a crow or two hovering over the same spot, and obviously not going away from there; or, again, if they stay perched on a tree for a long time. The shepherd is always needed then. He can be sure that the crows have spotted some weakness in the defences, and that they are just waiting the opportunity to pounce. They will fly around, their sharp eyes looking for some defenceless creature to attack.

Very often, when a ewe has delivered the first of twins, and while she is now concentrating on delivering the second, the crow sees its chance. With its great black beak it will pick out the eyes of the first from their sockets, or sometimes tear out its tongue or its entrails. This can happen to the ewe – the mother sheep – as well, despite her size, if she lies still and unwell for any length of time.

The carrion crow is reckoned the cleverest and most cunning of birds. There is no hope of getting near enough with a gun to frighten or destroy it. You can carry something resembling a gun on your shoulder, and the bird will make no attempt to move away. But a real gun it will know from afar, and be off without delay.

It is a wonderful thing that little lambs are able to survive those first hours of weakness, in spite of having so many enemies. How thankful they should be that they have a shepherd. Oh, that he could be present in many places at the same time!

We, too, should be thankful that we have a Shepherd, almighty and ever present, to watch over his 'born-again' and defenceless 'lambs', One who has conquered the power of the evil one.

4
THE STUBBORN SHEEP

It was sheer delight to be in Scotland, in Blair Athol, for the international sheep-dog trials. The wildness of the mountains, surrounding us in all their grandeur, seemed to be reflected in the behaviour of the sheep – sheep used to fighting the elements for their very existence.

I soon saw that handling the strong, black-faced sheep proved to be quite a test of the personality of the dogs, and it also tested more rigorously their under-standing and their obedience to the commands of their masters. The sheep immediately sensed any weakness in a dog, and took full advantage of it, especially towards the end of the long, hard course.

In the major competition for the championship, there were relatively few dogs that succeeded in penning the sheep, in spite of getting them to the door of the fold, which was waiting, wide open before them.

The shepherd did his best to coax them into the fold, though his freedom to do so was only the length of the rope fastened to the post of the fold, and his reach the length of his crook. The dog, too, under the insistent command of his master, did everything he could to persuade the sheep to give in and go through the door – this was one of the highlights of the course to which everyone looked forward.

For the most part, the stupid, stubborn sheep ran past the open door of the fold. They ignored it completely, as though it were not there. They had no interest whatsoever in the invitation to enter. Having refused to recognize the open door, and having passed it by several times, they would begin to push and huddle among themselves, one hindering the other, all heads and tails in the entrance.

Instead of making their way calmly through the opening, they were keeping a wary eye on the dog, looking for a chance to escape. A sudden, nervous leap, and off the sheep would go again, after so nearly being penned! You could hear the united groans of the crowd, in sympathy for master and dog, while away went the poor dog to make another effort to gather them back to the fold.

But, more often than not, I could see that, having begun to refuse, some obstinate hardness had possessed the sheep, which made them defy the shepherd and the dog. It was enough to make the onlookers feel that they might as well give up the struggle, even before the ringing of the bell, which signified that the time was up.

But it is not only Scottish sheep that can be obstinate. It is surely true that there is a hardness that can possess the human heart that persistently rejects God's offer of forgiveness through the death of the Lord Jesus Christ on the cross.

But once you have found yourself in the fold, though you have been shut in, joy will come from feeling and knowing that you are in the right place, a partaker of the freedom that comes from being in Christ and being a child of God. Although the fold is narrow, it is exceedingly deep.

'Seek the Lord while he may be found; call on him while he is near.'
    Isaiah 55:6

'Therefore God again set a certain day, calling it Today, when a long time later he spoke through David, as was said before: "Today, if you hear his voice, do not harden your hearts."'
    Hebrews 4:7

'The Lord is not slow in keeping his promise, as some understand slowness. He is patient with you, not wanting anyone to perish, but everyone to come to repentance.'
    2 Peter 3:9

5
FULL
MEASURE

It is a temptation to use the contents of some packet or tin, without reading and carrying out all the instructions carefully, whether it is food or medicine for man or beast. How easy it is to read the large print only, and satisfy oneself with that alone, perhaps to save oneself the bother of searching for one's glasses! But to ignore the smaller print can mean a heavy loss of time and money, and even life.

Every now and then, an order will come from the Ministry of Agriculture, telling us to dip every sheep within a specified period, and that in an exceptionally strong mixture approved by the Ministry. Its purpose is to destroy a disease in the skin of the sheep known as 'scab'.

Scab is caused by tiny mites, almost invisible to the naked eye. They live on the skin of the sheep, and it is easy for them to transfer from one sheep to another. When the sheep push their bodies against the overhanging banks, or some rock on the mountain, they leave traces of the scab there, for other sheep to pick up after them.

It is very important to obey the instructions carefully, as to how much water should be added to make the dipping effective. Some chemical specialists say that if the sheep are immersed several times in too weak a solution, the scab mites will sense that the water contains something that could endanger their lives, and they will gradually produce a protection that will enable them to resist the insecticide and render it harmless. And so, the scab mites will have a new lease of life and will continue to increase.

Sometime later, the shepherd, realizing the seriousness of the matter, may decide to immerse the sheep in a solution prepared to its full strength. But by this time the immersion has no effect on the scab mites. The effort is now useless, the disinfectant can no longer pierce the shell of their defence.

This is quite like our reaction if we are listen regularly to preaching which is diluted to please the age – a gospel which does not say much about repentance nor about sin and its results nor about the devil or hell.

Paul told the elders of the church at Ephesus: 'For I have not hesitated to proclaim to you the whole will of God' (Acts 20:27). He did that in *full measure* – and we know the consequences. Thank God, when the gospel is preached thus, and under the influence of the Holy Spirit, nothing can withstand this. Without such preaching, all sorts of spiritual mites will be able to live and increase.

6
THE DRAGON-FLY

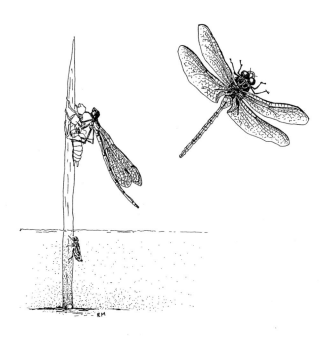

It was an exceptionally hot day. By raking the hay from the shadow of the hedge into the blaze of the sun, I was trying to justify my presence in the hayfield, though I was assured that the latest machines could easily clutch at that hay for themselves.

Before long, what should I see beside me but a dragon-fly, like some little fairy hovercraft. How glad I was to see it, not having set eyes on one for years.

It was a most beautiful creature, the colour of a duck's egg, which seemed to give the impression of shot silk, with its long body tapering to a point. Its four beautiful wings were like curtains of silky lace.

As I was beginning to feast my eyes on its beauty, it disappeared – just like a shooting star at night.

Suddenly, it returned with a swarm of similar creatures and flew round about me. Perhaps the hot sunshine had enlivened a nest of them in a deep ditch nearby. There was no more thought of hay-making for me – my eyes were riveted on them.

They hovered back and fore, as though they wanted a good look at me. They flew rather too close for my comfort. A flood of memories from childhood swept over me – and some of the fears as well. In those days, of course, I believed the old wives' tale that a dragon-fly had a sting like a bee or a snake, and I expect I gathered those beliefs from its Welsh name, *gwas y neidr* ('snake's servant'). Going home from school, we would go out of our way to avoid the spot where we had seen them last.

But now, knowing differently, it was sheer pleasure to gaze on their beauty, and see them flying and gliding in the air.

It was difficult to believe they had once been maggots, living in the mud and mire of some ditch or pond, one of the chief enemies of the tiny inhabitants there. The dragon-fly maggot plays havoc with, and destroys everything within its reach. Its fellow-insects live in terror of it; it is the very epitome of selfishness.

As it develops, the time comes to leave its watery, muddy world and climb up a reed to the surface. There it waits to dry its body and then unpack its wings before eventually flying for the very first time above the mire, a new splendid creature, a flash of colour in the sun.

The dragon-fly came out of the mire and was born

into a new world at exactly the right time. In doing so, it said 'farewell' for ever to its old life, and the old way of living, never again to return. It had exchanged it for a beautiful and pure environment.

'Unless a man is born of water and the Spirit, he cannot enter the kingdom of God.'
John 3:5

'Therefore, if anyone is in Christ, he is a new creature; the old has gone, the new has come!'
2 Corinthians 5:17

Hail the heaven-born Prince of Peace!
Hail the Sun of Righteousness!
Light and life to all He brings,
Risen with healing in His wings.
Mild He lays His glory by,
Born that man no more may die,
Born to raise the sons of earth,
Born to give them second birth.
CHARLES WESLEY

7
LIGHT

Who among us can say that a little back-scratching does not come amiss at times? Perhaps that is how the young tree felt when the first tendril of ivy began to creep up and cling to its trunk. Perhaps it welcomed it at first, perhaps appreciated its company! Little did it know at the time what was in store.

The tree became more conscious of the presence of the ivy as it felt its roots gradually penetrating the bark. As the ivy snakes its way up, its evergreen leaves spread like a mantle over the leaves of the supporting tree. There is a gradual inch by inch take-over, until in time more of the ivy can be seen than the tree itself.

Soon the sunlight cannot penetrate the thickness of ivy leaf to reach the leaves. In addition, the tree discovers that its leaves cannot breathe any more. And that is the beginning of the end. Its days are numbered.

All green plants have their life support from two sources. The roots derive nourishment from the soil, and the leaves breathe in carbon dioxide from sunlight. The tree turns these elements into supporting nutrients. But both soil and sun are essential. Even if roots prosper, all plants die if denied light.

Near us in Ceunant y Felin ('Mill Gorge') there are examples of tall, strong trees having fallen headlong, all dead wood. Once ivy gets a hold it respects neither strength nor beauty. The tree now has no value or use, except as firewood perhaps. But, ironically, when the dead tree falls, in one tangled mass, it brings down the ivy too.

The Evil One tries to take over our lives, offering pleasure and happiness. Sin is anything that seeks to rule our lives, apart from the Lord Jesus Christ. It may be drugs, the lust of the flesh, or materialism or just plain self-centredness – anything that allures and enslaves. Its purpose is to bring us down or to spoil our usefulness to God. It seeks to stop the light of heaven shining upon us lest we realize the truth about ourselves and our sin. Thank God for the miracle of grace which has the power to break into our lives and shine in our darkness.

Sanctify us, Lord, and bless,
Breathe Thy Spirit, give Thy peace;
Come and dwell within each heart,
Light, and life, and joy impart.

CHARLES WESLEY

Jesus said:

'I have come into the world as a light, so that no-one who believes in me should stay in darkness.'
    John 12:46

Jesus sent Paul to the Gentiles
'to open their eyes and turn them from the power of Satan to God, so that they may receive forgiveness of sins and a place among those who are sanctified by faith in me.'
    Acts 26:18

8
A MATTER OF BACKGROUND

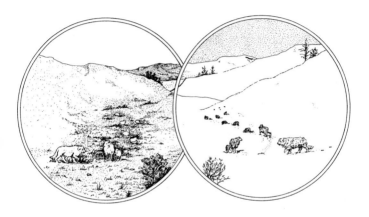

'No, it is too clear; the sheep over there on the other side are showing up much too well.' These are words often heard on our farm-yard when we want to discover the kind of weather we may expect. There are many activities on a farm when fine weather is an absolute necessity, and that is the reason why the weather signs are so carefully studied.

It is a bad sign when the mountains appear too close, and the sheep across the valley are too evident. At such times they appear like white spots, against the green of their background, or the copper of the dead bracken, or the blue grey of the rocks. Their background shows up their whiteness to all who see them.

When winter comes, it is a familiar sight of a morning to see the mountain, directly opposite us, white in its blanket of snow. The sheep show up just as well then, too, but no longer as white spots, but like dusky smudges against their dazzling white background. One could swear that they had changed colour overnight. How did they lose their whiteness so suddenly?

One of our dogs, Rhys, is a white sheep-dog, and his whiteness is very often a drawback in his work, so difficult is it to distinguish him from the sheep. When he gets the command to gather the sheep together, they think, from his colour, that he is one of them, and they are not convinced until he produces a sound, very different from the bleating of a sheep, and shows them his strength and his mastery over them.

But, when the yard is covered in new, dazzling snow, Rhys's colour too turns to a kind of dirty yellow, and it is difficult to restrain oneself from giving him a good wash in soap and water to find out, at the same time, whether it is true that 'whiter than white' is a possibility!

In northern countries, the stoat will change its colour according to its environment, and in winter it can be seen as white as the snow around it, while for the rest of the year its coat is the rusty brown of the mountain bracken. The secret of its safety is its ability to melt into its background. The sheep do not need this kind of safeguard, nor does Rhys the dog.

The whiteness of the snow shows the true colour of Rhys and the sheep, so that we marvel at the difference. The Holy Spirit alone will show us our true colour against the holiness of God; and the forgiveness of God alone will make us 'whiter than snow'.

'Have mercy on me, O God, according to your unfailing love; according to your great compassion

blot out my transgressions. Wash away all my iniquity and cleanse me from my sin . . . Cleanse me with hyssop, and I shall be clean; wash me, and I shall be whiter than snow.'
  Psalm 51: 1-2,7

'Make every effort . . . to be holy; without holiness no-one will see the Lord.'
  Hebrews 12:14

9
ESTRANGEMENT

If it looks like rain, and we are due to be shearing the next day, the sheep are all collected from the mountain the evening before. The ewes and the lambs come into the fold together, in tightly-knit couples. Then the lambs are separated and taken away, leaving only the woolly sheep

under cover. This is done because the wool must be dry for shearing, for it can become yellow and stained and spotted if it is left damp.

And, oh! what a heart-breaking protest is set up when the sheep and lambs are separated! The plaintive bleating of the ewes and the lambs can be heard all evening – the highpitched cry of the lamb, answered from afar by the deep bleating of the mother.

The colour and condition of the sheep's wool before shearing say quite a lot about their life during the past year – for instance the tell-tale colour which tells the shepherd that they have been rubbing themselves in the hollowed-out banks of the stream. The state of their coats tells, too, whether they have had a hard year. If they have suffered badly, the 'fibre' – the thread or filament nearest the skin – gets very thin. And later on, as the sheep improves in health and condition, this wool will break away. This is why sheep in this condition will sometimes lose much of their wool, and perhaps indeed, the whole of it before the shearing. It is an exception to find a flock where some do not show some signs of having a hard year.

And now the sheep, having been relieved of the dirty old mantle, are transformed. But one must admit that having lost their old garments, they do look thin and not much of a sight. They now look just as they are. They no longer have anything to cover their weak points. But they are white and clean and their master's brand-mark stands out plain and clear, to show to whom they belong. We also should make sure that the mark of our Saviour is distinctly seen on us, a clear evidence of our ownership.

At last they are set free to join their lambs. After all the noise the previous evening, you would expect the reunion to bring great rejoicing. But no! On the contrary, the noisy bleating goes on – the mother searching for her lamb, and when she has found him, the lamb refusing to acknowledge his mother! Though he knows her bleat, this clean white coat is causing grave doubts. No, this is not the mother that has nurtured him, not the mother that he has suckled and followed zealously for so many weeks. He tries to find the heavy smell of the dirty old coat that he knew so well. The bleat and the smell must correspond to each other. It will take time before he can accept this so different mother.

The same thing can happen, too, when the lamb is put through the waters of the dipping tub to cleanse and disinfect it. This time, it is the mother that does not recognize her lamb! She refuses to recognize him and a certain estrangement arises between them.

Many parents go through an similar experience, when one of their children goes through the 'washing' of the second birth, casting off the old clothing and putting on the new (Colossians 3:9-10). An estrangement, a tension comes into the hearth and home. The explanation is the same; they reject their child because he is different from what he was before, and because they themselves are, as yet, without this same experience.

Then, at other times, the children, like the lambs, are themselves unable to recognize their parents, when they, the parents, receive the forgiveness of God for the first time, and are made new creatures. The same can also happen between husband and wife. Great patience and tolerance and love are needed at such times.

10
THE ROWAN TREE

Many years ago a fine pine tree, growing at the foot of a hillock below our farm house, was felled. It was sawn some six feet above ground. Some time later a bird must have decided to use the stump's flat surface as a dining table. Its menu that day comprised of some rowan berries, and doubtless it enjoyed its meal. It left the rowan stones behind.

Before taking leave of the spot it seems that it made further use of its convenience! The stones were thus surrounded by natural, organic manure which encouraged them to throw out roots and upward-growing shoots. The slowly rotting pulp of the old tree, plus some loam which somehow found its way there, provided an ideal compost mixture for the rowan shoot to grow.

Over the years and in such favourable conditions, it has become a fine sapling, strong and sturdy because its roots reach down through the old growth into the soil below.

Every time I pass by I am reminded of Isaiah 11:1, 'A shoot will come up from the stump of Jesse; from his roots a Branch will bear fruit.' The prophet, of course, had Jesus Christ, the Messiah, in mind; he would be the 'shoot' and the 'Branch', since he would be the descendant of King David, the son of Jesse.

When September comes and the orange-red berries appear, how lovely is their brilliant colour. And we are reminded of another description of the Messiah, by the same prophet, that of the 'suffering Servant' who shed his blood and gave his life for us on the cross (Isaiah 53).

'To him who loves us and has freed us from our sins by his blood . . . to him be glory and power for ever and ever! Amen.'
    Revelation 1:5-6

11
LAYING A HEDGE

A hedge allowed to grow as it pleases, its branches reaching out aimlessly in all directions, is not only unsightly, but useless. So much energy is expended by a loose, untidy, upward growth, that the base of the hedge soon becomes so weakened that young lambs may be tempted to push their little bodies through the gaps and go astray.

Riddled with holes and weak spots, the hedge can no longer afford the animals sufficient protection from the summer's heat or the winter's storms. A good hedge is a boon to the shepherd, especially when fodder is in short supply – it provides the sheep with a welcome shelter and helps conserve body heat.

When the dishevelled growth shows signs of getting out of hand, the hedger comes to the rescue. He arrives, in late winter or early spring, with a pile of stakes and a mallet or hatchet to drive them into the ground.

He also carries a sharp billhook and a pair of hedging gloves – thick leather gloves not unlike those worn by boxers. But he wears them, not to punch the unprotected parts of an opponent, but to protect his hands from the ravages of the blackthorn. The needle-sharp tip of the blackthorn is poison to the human body at all times but especially so in spring when the sap begins to rise. The thorn has threatened many a life.

The hedger begins by removing the old growth, branches that have seen better days but are now withered and worthless. They must be removed so that light and air can penetrate the bottom of the hedge. This will encourage new growth and enable the hedger to see clearly which branches need splitting so that they can be laid in position.

This tricky task he does with the sickle or billhook, cutting three-quarters of the way through the branch, as close to its base as possible. Great care must be taken not to cut deeper thus causing the vital sap to drain away instead of rising into the wood.

This done, the branch is carefully bent or laid, alternately with other branches, to form a closely interwoven pattern. This task calls for a master craftsman – it takes a skilled hedger to lay a hedge that will continue to grow. The younger the branches, the easier they are to bend and the more likely they are to survive and prosper.

Each branch that has been trimmed and laid can now be seen as an integral part of the complete design. It remains to drive in stakes to hold the branches in position while they are still weak. They will lie at an angle in a direction opposite to the finished hedge so as to prevent the branches from straightening up again. Within a few years, when the hedge has grown strong enough to support itself, the stakes may be removed.

Before long the new closely-woven growth will provide valuable shelter for both animals and birds, especially those small birds that have so many enemies, ever anxious to devour their eggs and their chicks. The Nature Conservancy Council does all it can to encourage the old craft of hedging and it has strongly condemned the destruction and removal of hedgerows. A hedge that has been laid justifies its existence and performs its role of guarding the occupants of the field it surrounds, keeping trespassers at bay, and providing refuge and shelter for its many 'tenants'.

In a way, we are similar to hedges. If we refuse to accept God's authority in our lives, and in the corporate life of our churches, we will not achieve the purpose of our existence. But, if we allow the One with the sickle in His hand to trim and direct us, we shall fulfil His purpose for our lives, to His eternal glory.

12
THE HAND OF THE SHEPHERD

When the sheep-folds or pens were built on our yard,
provision was made in them to separate the sheep, when
that became necessary. It consists of a door which opens
onto a narrow pathway leading from one of the pens.
Only one sheep or lamb can go along it at a time, and at
the end of the path there are two exits, one to the right
and the other to the left. But there is only one choice for
the sheep or lamb! As they negotiate the path, what will
decide their fate is the hand of the shepherd on the door,

opening one appropriate 'exit', and shutting the other. The choice does not lie with the sheep.

In this way strange sheep can be shed from the flock when that is necessary. It is so much less laborious than having to lift and deliver an armful of heavy sheep to its rightful place, and very much kinder on the sheep as well.

It is not quite so kind when it comes to separating the lambs, and taking them away from their mothers for the first time, a little lamb that has never before seen anything of the world except in its mother's company! It has been following its mother for weeks, and now it is following her up the path as closely and hopefully as ever. And the door is shut firmly in its face! A painful separation, indeed!

The same process is followed when separating the fat lambs that have been weighed on the scales. The under-weights have to be returned to the fields, in the hope that by the time of the next weighing they will have added to their size. And the fate of that fat lamb that had followed its mother so faithfully? The slaughter-house I'm afraid.

It must be admitted that, sometimes, a mistake is made. For instance, the shepherd may be late in noting the brand-mark on the sheep, and consequently opens or shuts the wrong door. When this happens the sheep must have a second opportunity of going through the separating pen, and so be directed to its right place.

Sadly, the day of separation must come to every one of us; in the hour of death, for instance, when we, too, shall be cruelly separated from our dear ones by the hard, pitiless blow, dealt by the 'King of Terror', and still more dreadfully, on the great day of final separation. And it will be the hand of the Shepherd that will be on the door at that time too. The hands that bled for us on the cross of Calvary will do the separating.

Our comfort and hope lie in the fact that the Good

Shepherd is calling His sheep today. What right have those who reject him (or – which is just as bad – who wilfully push in among his sheep while not really belonging to Him) to protest or complain when they go through the separating pen and find the door shut?

One thing is certain – He will not make a mistake. He knows His sheep from afar, His brand-mark is plainly to be seen on them. And how final is the verdict! When that day dawns it will be too late to speak of a second chance. Jesus says:

> 'Moreover, the Father judges no-one, but has entrusted all judgment to the Son . . . I tell you the truth, whoever hears my word and believes him who sent me has eternal life and will not be condemned; he has crossed over from death to life.'
> John 5:22, 24

13
DAFYDD DAFIS

He was a short man, his trousers tied with string below his knees. Wearing a pair of meshed spectacles to protect his eyes, he sat straddling a heap of stones, one sack beneath him, another over his shoulders. That is my earliest recollection of Dafydd Dafis. At the time he was busy breaking stones, since part of his job as a road-man was to break large stones into smaller ones, suitable for filling pot-holes.

Although not renowned for the speed of his work, he excelled in thoroughness. When the foreman paid him a surprise visit one day he is reported to have said, with a touch of authority in his voice, 'Dafis, I would like to see that hammer lifted a little oftener.' 'It's the down-stroke that does the breaking, sir', the old road-man retorted.

He was slightly cross-eyed and more often than not there were streaks of tobacco-juice on either side of his mouth. Mind you, he only chewed his tobacco – he hadn't smoked since the Revival. Before that he had been a slave to alcohol.

Before his conversion he was barely literate, but he became so deeply affected by the heavenly Spirit that he longed to be able to read for himself what the Bible had to say about the One who had so dramatically changed his life.

At that time Dafydd Dafis worked on a farm and he thought nothing of getting up at half-past five on a Sunday morning to feed the animals, so that he could be in Sunday school by ten o'clock. There he learnt to read and he continued reading for the rest of his life, managing without glasses well into his eighties, much to everyone's astonishment.

He was made a deacon in the chapel at Parc, near Bala. 'Would you like to say a few brisk words to close the meeting, Dafydd Dafis?' the minister sometimes asked at the end of the weekly fellowship meeting. And whenever he opened his mouth, he had something well worth hearing.

If it was suggested, as sometimes happened, that he was over-confident of his salvation, he would be silent for a while. Then, possessed of a new certainty, and an authority so untypical of his meek personality, he would graciously say: 'Wasn't I there when it happened?' followed by a quiet chuckle. His crossed eyes sparkling, he would add, 'I have reason to believe that all will be well between me and the Almighty, if I settle my accounts with Him often enough. Keeping short accounts, that's the secret.'

I recall another fellowship meeting when someone said that we were all sinners, but that everything would be all right in the end since God is love, and Christ died for all. The usually placid Dafis got to his feet and, rapping the back of the pew in front of him with his fist, said with some feeling, 'No, you've got it all wrong. You forget that God is a just God and that each one must repent and receive His forgiveness for himself. That is how we are justified by Him, one by one – just as you go through the turnstile one by one into the show-ground.'

The vividness of his sayings scattered like quick-silver about our young ears. Dafydd Dafis's God was not some vague entity, but a personal, living God. Theirs was a warm, loving relationship.

He took great delight in repeating the sayings of some of the local 'characters' of the Revival. One of them was John Huws, whose love for the Saviour had been kindled in the 1859 Revival. On being asked by someone during the 1904 awakening why he did not rejoice as some others did, he replied: 'A lump of coal bursts into flame but once, from then on it gives out heat.'

His daughter and neighbours tenderly cared for him during his last illness. One Monday morning, on hearing how ill he was, a kind English visitor sent him a trout caught in the local river. A neighbour cooked it and took it to him, as he lay on his bed. He was enjoying his first mouthful, when he realized that the fish must have been caught on the Sunday. He spat it out. 'No, I can't' was his only comment.

Dafydd Dafis lived his life fearing the Lord and he died joyfully, unafraid of meeting Him.

14
ARAN
MIST

It was a day in late Autumn and I had last seen the four intrepid climbers that morning, setting out on the climb from the top of Bwlch Oerddrws, a high pass on the main road between Dinas Mawddwy and Dolgellau. Their parting words had been, 'Remember to be in the house around half-past three.' They intended climbing past Llyn y Figyn, over Aran Fawddwy, on towards Aran Benllyn and then down to Llanuwchllyn. I was to meet them there as soon as I received the phone call.

Seawards the sky looked rather pale, a few wisps of mist clinging to the highest slopes. One can never be sure what mist will do. It may lift or it may come down. And that day it came down.

As the four approached the summit of Aran Fawddwy the mist around them was like a blanket. Lower down had come across a local shepherd who was gathering his sheep, and he it was who directed them to the top. They knew that they had reached the top when they saw the expected cairn of stones.

In spite of the mist, they decided to head for Aran Benllyn, since they already had the advantage of being at the same altitude on Aran Fawddwy. It was an opportunity too good to miss. An hour's walk along the ridge and they should be on Aran Benllyn. And so they set off confidently through the mist.

When they had walked some distance one of the four commented that the cold had shifted from one cheek to the other. The implications of the remark were carefully weighed. The wind must have changed direction!

An hour went by, two hours, but still no sign of Aran Benllyn. Although now full of doubt and apprehension they had no choice but to continue walking. The two that had taken it upon themselves to be the leaders felt as hopeless and as helpless as the others. But they dare not confess it, not even to themselves.

At home, I was extremely worried. By now it was five o'clock and night was beginning to close in. There had been no phone call. I consoled myself as best I could; at least there was a doctor amongst them.

About that time, it transpired, there suddenly loomed ahead of them, out of the mist, a heap of stones. 'At long last,' said one of the four (undoubtedly, with a deep sigh of relief). But after a moment's consideration, he asked, 'Since when has there been a cairn on the summit of Aran Benllyn?' It was the doctor, giving an empty orange-can an almighty kick, who disconsolately remarked, 'I have a

feeling that I've been here before . . . today!' They were back on top of Aran Fawddwy!

What a blow this was to the pride of the pair who thought they knew the way so well! An ordinary map, had they even thought of taking one, would have been of no help at all in mist. But a map with a compass would have given them their bearings and the events of the day would have taken a totally different turn.

We live in a very mixed-up age, the mist of materialism so thick about us that it dims our political, moral, and spiritual vision. Oh that we would use God's authoritative Word as our map and let the Holy Spirit's infallible compass interpret it and show us our path, so that we might glorify the Lord and magnify His name at all times.

15
BROOM HILL

Calling the small hillock that rises between our
farmhouse and the village of Llanymawddwy Boncyn
Banadl ('Broom Hill') seemed to make hardly any sense

at all. It was once covered with tall sturdy pines and a variety of other evergreen trees. They had been there since time immemorial, nothing much growing beneath them save a thick carpet of ground ivy. Why, then, the romantic name 'Broom Hill'?

When they were about seventy years old, the trees were felled. They were dragged helter-skelter down to a nearby saw-pit to be cut into timber lengths, the branches put aside for burning. As a result of this frantic activity the surface of the ground was harrowed and churned up.

At that time, planting new trees to replace the old was not compulsory, and nature was allowed to take its course to provide the bare hillock with suitable cover. Much to everyone's astonishment, before very long the ground was clad with clumps of yellow broom. The seeds had been dormant all those years, waiting for favourable circumstances in which to germinate and grow.

Now that the ground had been loosened, the light and warmth of the sun could penetrate the soil around them and the seeds sprang into life. For many years they had waited patiently for this hour. They could do nothing themselves: external factors essential for growth were absent. But now, once more, 'Broom Hill' was living up to its name. It had regained its former splendour.

But we were not to enjoy the golden mantle for long. Growth of a very different kind soon pushed its way out into the light, supplanting and choking the yellow bushes. This was stronger and slower-growing, and little by little the meaning of the hillock's name disappeared once more. The slopes are now covered with willows, with many a silver birch among them.

Therein lies another mystery – from where had these last seeds come. Were they deposited there by the process of dispersal or did they too, like the broom seeds, lie dormant, waiting for suitable growing conditions, but needing a longer time to germinate because of their stronger growth. Be that as it may, there they are, a visible proof that nature proceeds according to her laws.

Similarly, the seed of the gospel prayerfully sown in the hearts of men and women over many years can lie dormant, waiting for favourable growing conditions. Only the light and warmth of the Holy Spirit can cause that seed to germinate and spring to life. How important it is that we continue steadfast in prayer and faithful in witness, so that the ground will be loosened and made ready.

> 'So is my word that goes out from my mouth. It will not return to me empty, but will accomplish what I desire and achieve the purpose for which I sent it.'
>   Isaiah 55:11

16
HIS MASTER'S WILL

There's a great deal of truth in the old Welsh proverb, 'A dog's ten years is a man's hundred.' It is especially true of a working dog whose whole life is spent doing its master's bidding. The continual round of gathering sheep from the mountain slopes takes its toll; the wear and tear on the heart shortens its life-span. But a good dog would sooner be run off its feet than be relegated to a lingering existence in the farmyard. The lap-dog, that has never strayed very far from its warm basket, stands a far better chance of achieving longevity.

Once that instinctive attraction to sheep has been aroused in a young dog, the mere sight of a flock makes it excited. Reverting to the habits of its ancestor, the wolf, it rushes into their midst. It may start tugging at their wool or, worse still, get a taste of blood, which can be the beginning of worse things to come. A young dog which has not been trained and disciplined must be kept under constant control, especially at lambing time.

The shepherd tames an over-excited dog by getting it accustomed to the sight of sheep. A number of ewes are put in a make-shift pen, made with poles and pig-netting, in a field. It is quite a test for a lively dog to be satisfied with just watching them. If only it could run among them, scattering them in all directions!

Dogs differ in temperament, each having its own 'personality'. The master must be aware of this and plan its training accordingly. If a sensitive dog is disciplined too severely its confidence may be undermined and it will become shy and fearful. It would take a lot of skilful therapy to delete the pain of such an experience. Like the proverbial elephant, the dog has a long memory.

A strong-willed dog has to be allowed a certain amount of scope to express its natural tendencies. It is a joy to watch it, unbeknown to itself, being gradually cajoled through love and persuasion to submit its will. (I should add that training a dog is one of the best tests of a shepherd's temper and patience, as he watches it doing the silliest things when, by then, it should know better.)

It would seem that a dog trained to obey its master has no choice henceforth but to act according to his will. It lives to please him: that is the purpose of its existence and it has complete self-satisfaction at the same time. Being so completely submitted, it no longer knows the difference between its own will and that of its master. The two have become one.

The dog has no way of knowing what plan its master has in mind, but by obeying his every command it will be perfectly fulfilled. And so it is with the Christian and his Master.

Take my will, and make it Thine;
It shall be no longer mine.
FRANCES RIDLEY HAVERGAL

17
JEALOUSY

Jealousy is particularly prevalent among animals. They make no effort whatsoever to hide it and seem utterly unashamed of their behaviour. The unwritten law of their kingdom is the survival of the fittest.

The robin's splendid isolation during the winter

months proves how effectively it guards its patch. Granted, it has no legal right to that territory, but woe betide any other robin that steps over its invisible boundary!

Nothing pleases a sheep-dog more than the honour of being asked by its master to help him with a special task. On the other hand, a dog not trained to do pair-work will take great offence if asked to work with another dog. Sharing its master's favours with another – no thank you! Its response is usually the canine equivalent of 'You can do it yourself!' Back to the farmyard it goes, its tail between its legs, and no amount of persuasion will bring it back.

But it is in the context of sex that this jealousy among animals becomes most pronounced. However soundly we might be sleeping, if one of our bitches is on heat we will know the very moment a strange dog enters the yard. Our own males will raise a fierce protest against the trespasser. And should the hopeful suitor dare pay a visit during daylight hours it will soon have to turn tail and beat a fast retreat!

Many a bloody battle has been fought between rival rams in autumn. (Mountain sheep are in season for only a certain period of the year.) Taking a few backward strides, the rams charge at speed until their heads knock together with a resounding crack. This procedure is repeated until one withdraws, but, occasionally the story is one of mortal combat.

When, by chance, two bulls confront one another, they are merciless and unyielding, especially if they happen to be fairly equally matched.

Pride and jealousy combined can be very costly; so strong is the urge to win that neither considers the benefits of the coward's way out.

Jealousy raised its ugly head very early in the history

of mankind. It underlies the sad stories of Cain and Abel (Genesis 4), Miriam and Moses (Numbers 12), and the same is true down the ages. And was it not envy that drove the Jews to persecute the Lord Jesus. 'For he knew that it was out of envy they had handed Jesus over to him' (Matthew 27:18).

But, unlike the animal, man has a conscience, and can repent. And in Christ's forgiveness, love is shed abroad in his heart.

'Love does not envy.'
1 Corinthians 13:4

18
THE HEN
AND HER CHICKS

When fertile eggs have been kept at the correct
temperature in an incubator, or when a broody hen has
been sitting on a clutch for three weeks, one can expect to
hear one gentle tap after another on one of the shells,
until, eventually, the tip of a chick's beak appears through
a hole. Soon we can expect the same with all the other
eggs. The tip of a chick's beak is shaped like a miniature
pick-axe to enable it to pierce the hard shell. Once it has
served its purpose it falls off.

What a joy it is to watch the emergence of new life! For a short time nothing seems to be happening. Then another slight movement and more of the chick's head comes into view. Then a bigger piece of shell falls away and soon the chick is half way out.

This is the time when, unable to contain our impatience, we might be tempted to give a little help by peeling away the shell. But by doing so we could so easily hurt the chick, and cause bleeding, which would hardly be a kindness. There is 'a time to be born'; we must let nature take its course.

The chick that has struggled and fought its own way out will be that much stronger to meet the hazards of life. We have to accept that there is no birth without pain. And if the eggs have been hatched by a hen, she will do her utmost to prevent anyone from interfering. 'Leave us alone!' she will noisily protest. Many a time was I pecked before I learned my lesson.

Soon after the chicks have hatched, the proud mother will be seen strutting across the farmyard showing off her new family, tiny fluffy balls of yellow scurrying around beside her.

It is interesting to listen to the different calls the hen uses to communicate with her chicks.

Having scratched and searched the ground with her feet, on discovering a tasty morsel, a worm perhaps, she will cut it into small pieces and then excitedly summon her little ones to come and feast together on the delicacy. In no time at all they will be there, each anxious to be the first to arrive.

Another time, when the busy little bodies are weary after a spell of foraging, the mother hen will call them to take a welcome siesta. Her wings spread out on the ground, with her soft clucking she gently persuades her little ones to hide beneath them. They gladly respond and rush to snuggle up in the warm comfort of her feathers. (But invariably there will be the inquisitive individual that will poke its head between the quills lest it should miss something that is going on in the wide world outside!)

But when the hen senses the proximity of a bird of prey or some other threat to her little ones, her call has that distinctive tone that conveys her alarm. It is a stern command to come without delay and take cover under her wings; it demands swift response. And woe betide the chick which turns a deaf ear, or the one which has strayed too far to hear the call.

We may marvel at the hen's care for her brood, but it is only a pale reflection of the heavenly Father's love for those who obey his call to repent and come to Him in faith. And when they come they receive all that they need: food, rest, shelter and safety.

Our Lord's words as He looked down on Jerusalem are a solemn warning to the church today. 'O Jerusalem, Jerusalem, you who kill the prophets and stone those sent to you, how often I have longed to gather your children together, as a hen gathers her chicks under her wings, but you were not willing!' (Luke 13:34; Matthew 23:37).

'You were not willing!' What an awful indictment! But if we respond to God's call, our souls will be in His safe-keeping both now and for ever. How can we refuse such a gracious offer!

> 'How priceless is your unfailing love! Both high and low among men find refuge in the shadow of your wings.'
> Psalm 36:7

> 'Keep me as the apple of your eye; hide me in the shadow of your wings.'
> Psalm 17:8

'He will cover you with his feathers, and under his wings you will find refuge; his faithfulness will be your shield and rampart.'
Psalm 91:4

19
THE STING

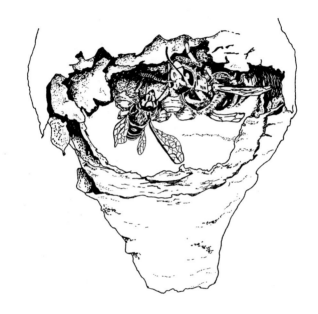

The moment I felt a sudden painful prick on my neck, I knew I had been stung. At the time I could think of no remedy other than the old-fashioned one of applying wet washing blue.

While I was busily dabbing the sore spot, I tried to imagine what kind of wasp the culprit could have been, there being none there to confess to the dread deed!

Was it, perhaps, one of those potter or mason wasps that spend their lives in splendid solitude? And was it

suddenly so overwhelmed by a craving for companion-
ship that it honoured me with its overtures?

I have read that it builds its nest of clay pellets stuck
together with saliva. The finished work resembles a
round vase which tapers at the top into a slender bottle-
neck. This is attached to twigs or other suitable objects.

The wasp permanently paralyses and immobilizes a
certain species of caterpillar by stinging it, and then drags
it into the nest. Then it lays its egg, suspending it by a
silken thread of its own manufacture three-quarters down
from the opening. Finally it seals that opening with more
clay pellets.

When the egg hatches the wasp larva feeds to
maturity on the paralysed caterpillar, and it soon becomes
strong enough to bore its way through the nest wall into
the big world outside. Before long it, too, starts building a
nest, as independent as ever its parent was. Another
lonely cycle is set in motion.

Or could that stinger have been a stray member of a
colony which co-operate to build their nest? Their effort
produces a masterpiece of grey silk which can be found
hanging from the rafters of outbuildings or in hedgerows. The men come across them unexpectedly when
hedge-trimming in autumn. Woe betide them if, in-
advertently, they 'disturb the peace' – the sooner they run
for the shelter of the tractor-cab the better! The wasps
will soon let them know on whose territory they are
trespassing.

In autumn bees and wasps often keep us company as
we pick fruit or prepare it for cooking and preserving,
and, more often than not, they will let us know that they
resent sharing the spoils. Their presence does detract
somewhat from the pleasure of that 'season of mists and
mellow fruitfulness'.

As insects, they are especially interesting and

beautiful. Oh, that they might be deprived of their sting so as to give us a better chance to appreciate and examine their sleek form.

The Scriptures tell us that 'the sting of death is sin' (1 Corinthians 15:56). But having received forgiveness and cleansing from God, we can face death without fear and say with the apostle Paul,

' "Where, O death, is your victory?
    Where, O death, is your sting?"
The sting of death is sin, and the power of sin is the law. But thanks be to God! He gives us the victory through our Lord Jesus Christ.'
1 Corinthians 15:55-57

20
POWER CUT

'Leave that electric fire on!' That was the usual word of command at one time, given in order that the said fire should take the load of electricity generated by the turbine.

At that time the water of the stream was used – the stream that ran down the valley without aim or purpose, almost wastefully. A dam had been built across the stream to divert the course of the water to the intake, which was covered by a grating. Through this ran the water, the full force of it directed to a pipe which led, through a drop of some five hundred feet, to the turbine. Channelling the water in this way gave it a great increase of pressure and power to drive the turbine, which turned the dynamo that generated our electricity.

Those were prodigal days, days of useless waste: sometimes the whole output had to be used – or wasted! – in case the dynamo should be burnt out. They were also pleasant days, with no anxiety about possible electricity bills in the offing! How different it is today! 'Turn that heat off as soon as you can' is the order of the day now.

However, there was no certainty about the supply of electricity in those days either. With the coming of floods, with the water rising, rubbish would be swept downstream bringing bracken and gravel and grit, and perhaps an occasional plastic bag, to the grating. This would impair the supply of water to the pipe and as a result reduce our supply of electricity. This meant fumbling around the house in semi-darkness, and once the rubbish started accumulating, more and more would be added to it, so that sooner or later we would be cast into inky blackness.

At such times, if Dr Martyn Lloyd-Jones were staying with us and there was no electricity for his razor, 'Whiskers again!' was his cry, with a mischievous smile at the thought of having a satisfactory reason for not shaving! And there we would be, in darkness, while the water ran unchannelled, purposeless and ineffective. Yes, and in darkness we would remain until someone went to clear the rubbish from the grating. Once this was done and the way was open again, what a rush the water made for the pipe – you would think it was in a race for first place! And as for the noise the pipe made as it swallowed the renewed flow, you would think it was gargling!

Even quite a small branch across the mouth of such a pipe, gathering increasing shreds of rubbish to itself continually, can hinder the drainage, causing the water to flood and ruin a field. There is a well-known riddle which asks, 'What goes more swiftly when its head is cut off?' No, not bracken and not a cockerel, but the rush of water when the obstruction blocking the head of a ditch is removed. One has but to remove the blockage – perhaps an offending turf – and immediately the ditch seems to gather up the water with all its strength and send it with all its power and energy on its course.

A failure to clear away anything which comes between us and the Lord can be just like the accumulation of rubbish at the pipe-head: it can hinder the flow of spiritual power into our lives, dull the reality of our Lord's presence and cast us into spiritual darkness.

> *Take from my soul all, high or base,*
> *That checks the flow of heavenly grace.*
> WILLIAM WILLIAMS, PANTYCELYN (tr.)

Let us remember, however, that we are speaking of those who are already Christians, to whom Jesus Christ is Lord. As for others, before they can experience the flow of living waters into their lives, it is not a 'small branch' or some bracken that must be removed, but a whole life's accumulation of sin.

21
THE RED KITE

'Keep an eye on the nest in that tree over there?' The time was early spring, and the man speaking to John was a member of the Royal Society for the Protection of Birds. We did not know at the time that a pair of red kites had nested in one of the trees nearby.

He went on, in order, no doubt, to boost John's enthusiasm, to enlarge upon the fact that the kite was second to none as a hunter, and a hunter over a wide area at that. Moreover, in the spring, as a rule, crows' chicks will be high on the kites' menu, and the man was not slow in suggesting to John that these might be the very chicks that would be pulling out and eating the eyes and the tongues of next year's lambs!

But the scarcity of the birds, of course, was the chief reason for guarding the nest. Nowhere in the British Isles will you, today, find the kite nesting, except in mid-Wales. At the beginning of this century it nearly became extinct, but found a refuge in Wales, and by this time its numbers are on the increase – although, unfortunately, the kites which nested on our land have left.

What a beautiful bird the kite is! When the sun shines directly on it, you would think it was made of copper or bronze. In this country it is, of all the birds, the nearest in size to the eagle. Its tail is forked like that of a swallow – that is what distinguishes it from the buzzard with its fan-like tail. It is a joy to see the kite on the wing, gliding, rather than flying, slipping through the air so smoothly and effortlessly. Many a bird's flight is a trifle clumsy as it flaps its wings with seemingly too much effort to stay aloft, but not so the red kite. How often are we guilty of 'flapping' in a flurry of self-effort rather than trusting and being carried above our circumstances.

In the vicinity of the nest, we have watched, with the greatest interest, many a one-sided aerial battle between the kite, possibly newly returned from a murderous visit to the nests of the crows, and these same crows now in vindictive mood, bent on retaliation. They would nose-dive the kite, while it would ignore them completely and merely weave its way through them.

While the persecution and the protest are taking place, the broody hen will sit calmly on her eggs nearby. In the midst of all the noise, the new life within the eggs is quietly and consistently growing, and taking more and more room inside the shell. In about a month's time, this new life will push its way out of the eggs – all in its own good time. What a bustle followed the appearance of the two chicks, with their parents kept busy feeding them with something easy to digest at first, and stronger meat to follow.

All this is very like the course of our spiritual history. It may be in the midst of noise and bustle around us that the Holy Spirit will bring to the birth a new life within. And then, in God's good time we are born again as His spiritual children, and begin to grow.

In time the young birds take to their wings, daring to leave the narrow confines of the nest for the endless freedom of the sky, to enjoy the limitless expanse of the firmament for as long as they keep the rules of the air! And as the chicks enjoy the freedom of the sky, so we may prove (if we obey His laws) the unfettered joys of the new life in Christ here and now.

'But those who hope in the Lord will renew their strength. They will soar on wings like eagles; they will run and not grow weary, they will walk and not be faint.'
Isaiah 40:31

22

BEING A FARMER'S WIFE

This article first appeared in *Y Wawr*, the magazine of the Welsh-language women's organisation 'Merched y Wawr'. It was one in a series of articles on the theme 'Being the wife of a . . .' It is published here by kind permission of the editor of *Y Wawr*.

Wonder of wonders, the unexpected click of the front door letter-box – the postman! He hasn't been here for three days! It's the second week in January and our lane has been filled with mountainous drifts of light snow blown by the wind and shaped like an unbaked meringue.

The 'Merched y Wawr' logo is on one envelope. What on earth could they want?

The editor of *Y Wawr* suggesting that I might contribute to the series 'Being the wife of a . . .' – a farmer in my case, of course. My first reaction was 'No, never!' But sitting by a grate full of blazing logs that evening I found myself thinking. What on earth can I say in the middle of winter like this for the summer issue of the magazine?

Well, I'll tell you what it meant being a farmer's wife last night.

My husband John had a nasty fall on the slippery snow in early evening – he fell flat on his back, both hands in his pockets. He couldn't lift his right arm so we immediately thought that he had injured his collar-bone. We would have to go and see the doctor in the morning.

There was no one else available, so I tried to help him by filling the buckets with mashed oats for feeding the calves. It was an easy task spreading it along the troughs, each Charolais calf and an occasional Welsh Black pushing its head through the bars for its share. Then I mucked out behind some of the cattle – all under John's eagle eye.

I felt so pleased! No, not that John had hurt himself, but that I could be of some help.

Then I fed the seven sheep-dogs. It's strange how each one knows its own tin. The three puppies were so excited that they waded through their supper, unable to get their heads into it soon enough.

Having left every animal in a dry, warm bed, we could so much the more enjoy our comfort by the fire and later under the electric blanket, in spite of the icy wind that whipped round the house.

Thankfully, by this morning John had greatly improved. We came to the conclusion that he must have damaged a nerve in his shoulder. My assistance would no longer be needed.

John got up early, cooked his porridge, adding the usual bran, sultanas, milk and honey. Now I've divulged the secret of the popularity of his porridge! No, he hasn't added salt for many a year. Then, a time of meditation which includes the reading of God's Word. At present he is much blessed reading *The Practice of the Presence of God* by Brother Lawrence. I also try to read and meditate likewise before getting up.

Both of us wish we had more time to meditate in his way, and that the time we do have meant more to us. The Lord must be given the opportunity to show us what He wants to do in our lives. Farming in this way can be quite thrilling.

We must not allow our thoughts to dwell on

yesterday's difficulties, nor on tomorrow's either – things like the wet summer and the restrictions caused by Chernobyl. Rather we shall let the heavy aroma of silage bales stripped of their black night-shirts remind us of the six glorious weeks we had in September.

Like all housewives, I spend most of my time preparing food. Plenty of healthy food, rich in vitamins, is a must for farmers like Hefin and John, who are out in the open air and need to be physically strong.

One day I prepare lamb's broth or lobscouse, throwing in as many different vegetables as possible; the following day I skim off the surface fat. The numerous cats we have love the taste of the greasy globules in their food and what a gloss it gives their fur!

It is not uncommon to see a figure appearing unexpectedly at the kitchen door, asking hopefully whether it's possible to have dinner that very moment – for five men! The mist perhaps has lifted, making it possible to gather the sheep from the mountain. Oh dear, what a job it is trying to rack one's brains and search the fridge for 'instant' possibilities at the same time! It's essential always to have a supply of cold meat and similar food to hand, not just in the icy safety of the freezer.

Sometimes, lifting my eyes from the kitchen sink, I have the pleasure of watching John trying to teach some young sheep-dogs to recognize various whistled commands. What joy it is to see them submit to his will. There can be nothing more useless on a farmyard than a dog which does not understand nor yield to its master's will; equally useless are our lives if we do not yield to the will of the Good Shepherd.

23
WHAT'S HAPPENING TO DAFYDD?

Monday, 26 March
The usual Monday morning rush for stockings and gloves.
A mad rummage for dinner-money and a running trot
down the path. Then a silence like the peace of the
mountain reigning in the kitchen.

Dafydd is out since early morning – the lambs baling
out like parachutes. They would stay where they were if
they knew how cold it is! The wind is from the east and as
cutting as a razor.

Papering the best bedroom all day. It's difficult to
think of summer in this cold, but soon after lambing ends
the visitors will start arriving. One must get the bedroom
ready for them.

Wednesday, 28 March
What weather! Heavy rain, cold all day. Dafydd had to
change at mid-day, he was soaked to the skin. He'd had to
catch a sheep to help it lamb. After the birth, the mother
took hardly any notice of it, the dogs had so annoyed her!

Usually the ewes lick their newly-born, swallowing
the after-birth and all – nature's way of recycling the
minerals and vitamins which the sheep has provided for
her developing lamb. How wonderfully nature looks after
her young ones! Dafydd took the lamb, a slimy yellow
bundle newly out of the womb, on his arm and drove the
ewe before him to the hayshed, hoping the two would
forge a bond when penned together.

As they approached the hayshed, the lamb gave a bleat, the very first bleat its little throat had produced. The ewe jerked to a halt, as though a clock had struck inside her, and looked longingly at the lamb in Dafydd's arms. The lamb was put down and its mother claimed it that very minute. She licked it; she allowed it to suck; it received the woolly mother's inheritance in its entirety. The scene caused Dafydd to wonder. How did the mother recognize the bleat?

Thursday, 29 March
Dafydd's been very strange lately! In the middle of breakfast he said that had not the lamb bleated, its mother would not have claimed it yesterday, and that God does not claim us unless we cry to Him, despite the fact that He is the author of that cry. Well, well! He sees a religious meaning in everything nowadays, ever since the service taken by those students in chapel the other Sunday.

I see too little of him these days to get him to explain anything. His life is a continuous round of work and sleep. Up early and out till late, skinning some dead lamb so that its skin can be used to cover a live one. The dead lamb's dam, sniffing the covered lamb, usually adopts it before the night's out, believing it to be her own. Dafydd can then turn them out of the pen, a close couple that have accepted each other.

Friday, 30 March
The weather has become warmer. From crack of dawn there has been a medley of bird song, the birds singing with all the passion of their being, trying to attract a mate. A short visit to Dolgellau market to get a supply for the freezer. Saw the first wagtail of the season. Everywhere carpets of golden daffodils.

The men have stumbled across an easy way of

getting a dead lamb's mother into the yard, to persuade her to adopt another – the dead lamb is dragged along the ground with a bale-cord and the ewe is allowed to sniff now and then to convince herself that it is hers. She will follow the scent all the way to the yard in one straight line for half a mile, so determined is an animal to claim its own. 'That is how God knows his own, his children', said Dafydd. Oh, not more religious talk!

Sunday, 1 April
I couldn't persuade this girl of ours to get up to go to chapel. What's wrong with young people today? *We* used to go to chapel. Their Saturday nights have overlapped their Sunday mornings and the two will not mix, no more than oil and water. Trying to reason with them is like pouring water on a duck's back. And Gwen had the cheek to say that she doesn't think our chapel-going makes much difference to us. Well! Children have no respect for parents these days.

But Dafydd made allowances for them. He said they belonged to a very honest generation, that today's young people were looking for reality, and that holding on to tradition for it's own sake did not appeal. He tried to explain what he meant, but I couldn't understand.

Anyway, I had little time to listen, as Kate and Emrys Jones were coming for tea. Their daughter Jane is getting married early in the summer. It will be a very posh affair – making up for their own wedding, I dare say.

March by now going out like a lion; a young lamb in the kitchen, half starved, its mother having abandoned it.

Monday, 2 April
The washing machine has broken down. What a wretched nuisance! Had to do the washing in the sink. A day of losses – two ewes, the mothers of twins, have died. It will

be difficult to find four sheep to take the orphaned lambs. Had to give them a bottle of cow's milk in the middle of washing. They insisted on gnawing the teat like chewing-gum instead of sucking it and swallowing. Talk about the patience of Job, I wonder what his wife's patience was like! There is certainly a lot of truth in the old Welsh saying, 'Buy a sheep and you buy trouble, yet buy a sheep.'

Wednesday, 4 April
A cold but sunny day. Mothers found for two of the pet lambs, less work for me. Did some gardening after dinner – it's hopeless waiting for the men. The only time you see them in the garden is when they're digging for worms to poison the moles!

The mole is an interesting creature. If you give the worm too much poison, when the mole swallows it, it vomits. Its stomach automatically reacts to the excess and it happily resumes its task of hill-making! You can get too much of a good thing.

Planted spring onions, beans and lettuce. Heavy rain during the evening. April weather is like a spoilt child: it doesn't know what it wants!

Friday, 6 April
It's been a bit of a shambles all day. Went to town with Dafydd in the Land Rover. Very little time to do the shopping as Dafydd wanted to go round the sheep before dark. No time to have a chat with anyone nor to have a cup of tea!

We nearly had an accident by Cae Foty on the way home. It's only when his eyes cross from a field on one side to a field on the other side that Dafydd sees the road at all! We nearly had a good row but he kept apologizing. How different he is from the way he used to be.

I can't but feel that something has happened to Dafydd lately. He's so gentle, and he sees a religious meaning in everything. What's more he's taken to reading the Bible every available moment – and at such a busy time as the lambing season!

He mustn't get too religious – it may affect his mind. I wouldn't want him to be different from the neighbours around us. They'll take him lightly, an object of fun. He's taking his religion far too seriously, dragging it into everything. Too much religion defeats its purpose, like giving moles too much poison. A little is all right. 'Too much pudding can choke a dog,' as we say.

Saturday, 7 April
Can't for the life of me forget the chat we had in bed last night. How Dafydd, being so tired, could stay awake, beats me. He was trying to tell me how 'the truth' (as he called it) had got hold of him.

He said that for some time he had longed for proof of the reality of God in his life, and for His forgiveness. What for, I don't know! He once thought that by living a good respectable life, and doing something for Christ, God would accept him. This spring it dawned on him that it was a matter of accepting what Christ had done for him on the cross, Christ's righteousness covering us in the same way as the dead lamb's skin covers a live one.

Because it had its scent, the live lamb is acceptable to the mother of the dead lamb. And so God, in His holiness, accepts only those that bear the fragrance of Christ's righteousness. He mentioned those lines from the hymn, 'Clothed in His righteousness alone, faultless to stand before the throne', and said that it was now true of him.

I couldn't sleep for a long time. Dafydd's words kept circling in my head like a merry-go-round. *I* can't see it at all, or I'm blind.

This afternoon Lisa called with Auntie Ann and a car full of people. They caught me as untidy as could be, in the middle of spring-cleaning, and without a cake in the house. 'Therefore be ye ready, for ye know neither the day nor the hour' when *visitors* might call! O yes, I too can quote verses of Scripture!

Sunday, 8 April
Well! A Sunday like any other Sunday, I suppose? We went to the morning service. As we sang, I caught a glimpse of Mr Jones the schoolmaster's wife's new suit. She must have paid a pretty penny for that smart hat, but it didn't suit her at all – the brim was too large. It's surprising what we women will wear in order to be 'with it'.

It's difficult to gather one's thoughts and keep them in the right track to listen; from the beginning of the sermon I was trying to work out how best to tailor last year's dress to suit this year's fashion. Beside me, Dafydd sat listening like a judge. During the communion I noticed him wiping a tear. He explained later that this was his first communion after seeing, like John Elias, that it 'was for my sin that Jesus suffered so'.

Did I say like any other Sunday? I don't know what's wrong with me tonight. I find it very difficult to know what's happened to Dafydd. And yet? Tears have never been that close to the surface in my life.

Why am I finding fault with myself? Am I beginning to see myself as He sees me, in His light?